The Strawberry Seeds

The Strawberry Seeds

The story of unconditional love

Ciera Fulcher

XULON PRESS

Xulon Press
2301 Lucien Way #415
Maitland, FL 32751
407.339.4217
www.xulonpress.com

© 2022 by Ciera Fulcher

All rights reserved solely by the author. The author guarantees all contents are original and do not infringe upon the legal rights of any other person or work. No part of this book may be reproduced in any form without the permission of the author.

Due to the changing nature of the Internet, if there are any web addresses, links, or URLs included in this manuscript, these may have been altered and may no longer be accessible. The views and opinions shared in this book belong solely to the author and do not necessarily reflect those of the publisher. The publisher therefore disclaims responsibility for the views or opinions expressed within the work.

Paperback ISBN-13: 978-1-6628-5100-1
Ebook ISBN-13: 978-1-6628-5101-8

Table of Contents

Introduction ix
How It All Started................................1
A Plus One or Two 17
Undeserving 27
Devastation 36
Switching Sides (Luke)—Part One................. 43
Switching Sides (Luke)—Part Two................. 50
Jumping Ahead (Mia) 57
Imperfect Dreams................................ 62
Digging Deep (Luke) 69
When the Lights Come On (Mia) 76
Pain Is Real 83
Joy after the Storm 88
The Strawberry Seeds............................91

Introduction

As I lay there resting in his arms, I couldn't help but to think about my family and how this could destroy everything if Luke finds out. Now I'm feeling guilty all over again. This is not the first time I have cheated on my husband, and I doubt it will be the last time. I know it's wrong, but at this moment, it feels so perfect and right. The crazy thing is that Luke and I will be celebrating our fifteen-year anniversary soon, and I don't really know how to feel about that. Let me take you back to the beginning of how it all started.

Chapter 1

How It All Started

My name is Mia Milton. My husband, Luke Milton, and I have been married for fifteen years. We were high-school sweethearts, having met freshman year in study hall. I was minding my own business when Luke sat next to me and introduced himself. I was focused on reading my book and jamming to my music, so I wasn't paying him any attention. He kept trying to make small talk, but I wasn't having it, so I completely ignored him. I think he got the picture because he left me alone after a week of being ignored went by. I would see Luke in the hallway during passing period, but he would be with random girls or with his bros. When he noticed me in the hallway, he would always wave, and the least I could do was wave back, so I did. One day, I needed some help with an assignment I was working on in study hall, so I asked Luke. From that point on, Luke and I started to talk more and became good friends. He introduced me to all his friends, and I introduced him to all my friends.

As time passed, we became closer, which was cool, but Luke was in a relationship. He had been with this girl, Avery, ever since eighth grade. Avery was super pretty, with beautiful hazel eyes, long, naturally curly hair, and a nice, hourglass shape. She was outgoing, on the dance team, and she knew a lot of people. I liked Avery, but she didn't like that me and Luke were friends. When they went to the school football games, Luke would always invite me along with them and their other friends, but it was me that Avery didn't want around. At the time I didn't quite understand why, but as time went on, I started to get it. Luke liked me.

Let me tell you how I found out. My friend Stacy was having a small get-together at her house for the weekend because her parents were out of town for business. So she invited me and our friend Kaley to be there with her for the weekend. Stacy's parents trusted us because they had been friends with my parents and Kaley's parents since

How It All Started

we were babies. Our parents were members of this local church, and that's how they met. They became friends, and we three girls became friends. Stacy was an only child like me, and Kaley had an older brother named Kyle; he was hot but off-limits because she was our best friend.

So that weekend we were at Stacy's house, and we were having some girl talk. That's when Kaley told me that Luke was crazy about me. I couldn't believe her because she loves joking around, but she was serious this time. Her brother, Kyle, was on the football team, and Luke was too. They became cool, and Luke told Kyle, and of course Kyle told Kaley. And that's how I found out. But the story gets even more juicy.

Since Stacy heard that, she decided to invite Luke and his two friends Danny and Ryan over. This was perfect for Stacy because she liked Ryan, and Kaley liked Danny. So that night they came over, and we watched movies; then we talked and played games. It was fun, but then Stacy asked everyone to play spin the bottle; it was Luke's turn, and guess where the bottled turned. On me of all people. I was in shock, that was our moment, and it was a great moment because he came and kissed me with the most passionate kiss ever. I thought I was dreaming!

The Strawberry Seeds

After the game we all went our separate ways for bed, Stacy and Ryan went to her room, and Kaley and Danny went to the guest room. Luke and I slept in the living room, but we didn't have sex; we just talked all night. We talked about everything from love to our passions, dreams, future children, and even college. We really became close that night. The boys left the next day, and then that evening Stacy's parents came home. We stayed another night, and then Kaley and I went home.

After that crazy fun weekend, Luke and I were inseparable. He would meet me at my locker in the morning and walk me to class, and then he would sit with me at lunch. He would also walk Avery to class when she wasn't with her posse. But most of the time, Avery was with her friends, so she didn't notice Luke. During summer break, Luke broke up with Avery, and he and I became closer. By the time sophomore year started, we were dating.

I had met his parents over summer break, and he met mine as well. My parents liked Luke from the moment they met him, and his parents liked me too. I also met Luke's little sister, Mary Anne, but she was a little mean. I was so excited to be with Luke, and all our friends were happy for us. We did everything together: we studied together, ate lunch together, and even had a few classes together. Avery found out we were dating and didn't like that. She started rumors about me, saying that I was fooling around with Luke the whole time they were together, and I was the cause of their breakup. I clearly wasn't. People started to notice me because of Luke, and she was jealous and wanted people to dislike me.

No one noticed me until I started dating Luke. I was considered the pretty, quiet girl. But that changed when I started dating Luke. People knew Avery was just trying to hurt me, so they just ignored her. Avery didn't like me and Luke together, so she decided to try to get him back, but he didn't want her back. Avery had cheated on Luke with an upperclassman during freshman year. When Luke found out, he forgave her, but she kept doing it, so he finally broke things off. So now Avery can't stand to see Luke with me.

I decided to ask Luke why he liked me so much when Avery was much prettier than me. Luke said I'm beautiful inside and out, I have a heart for people, and I am honest. He said that I am everything he wanted in a girlfriend and in a future wife. I was surprised to hear that; he made my day saying that. I just always felt like Avery was so pretty with her hazel eyes, and I just had simple, dark-brown eyes. She had long curly hair, and I had short wavy hair; she had a small perfect nose, and I had a nose (other people said it was small, but I didn't like my nose). She had a cute shape, and I was just skinny. But Luke saw more than that, and that's why I loved him.

By the time we got to our junior year, my parents were inviting Luke with us on trips, and his parents were inviting me on trips. We met each other's extended family, and it felt great. We even went with each other to tour colleges because we were planning on going to the same college. By the end of junior year, we had decided on a college together. It was a university that was forty-five minutes away from the city we lived in. We applied for the university, and both of us got accepted, so we were even more excited about our senior year.

Luke's parents bought him a car as an early graduation gift. He was thrilled the day he got it; I remember he came to pick me up to take me for a ride. It was a Jeep, something he had always wanted, and it was nice. Senior year finally started, and Luke decided to drive his car to school. The first day of school, he picked me up and started going in the direction of the school. Suddenly, Luke turned down a different street, but I assumed that he was going a different

How It All Started

way to school. Soon, I realized that we were headed to his house. As he entered his neighborhood, I began to wonder if he had forgotten something at home, but then he smiled and said, "I have a surprise for you." I knew something was up when I saw that charming smirk on his face.

Luke has this charming smile that gets me every time, and this time wasn't any different. I loved seeing that perfect smile with those perfect, round, soft lips. He had the cutest dimples that would appear even with the slightest smirk. As we were pulling up to this big, beautiful, empty house, I couldn't help but to wonder what he had up his sleeve. Luke's parents were lawyers, and their home was immaculate. Their house was big enough for a whole other family to live with them. I loved going to his house because it was so big. My parents' house was cute and small, so I wasn't used to anything big. But let's get back to the story.

Finally, Luke pulled into the driveway, turned the car off, got out, and then came around to the passenger side to let me out. I tilted my head up to look him in the eyes to see what he was doing, but I instantly saw that charming smile again. I knew what he was up to; Luke was planning on having sex. I began to feel butterflies in my stomach, and my mind started racing a million miles a minute. I was excited, nervous, scared, anxious, happy, worried, and everything else you can name. We had talked about sex plenty of times and how I wanted to wait until marriage. As time passed, Luke and I became more serious and eventually fell in love with each other. I finally decided that I wanted to lose my virginity with him before we graduated high school.

I guess Luke decided this would be the perfect moment, which was the *first day of school*! Luke wasn't a virgin; he lost his virginity to Avery when they were dating. I was nervous about that too because I wanted this to be better than his time with Avery. I know that was petty, but I was still in high school, so I was still childish. He also had sex with another girl the same summer that he broke up with Avery. I guess that chick was just a rebound because he never talked to her again after that. He said he met her while he was working at the mall that summer. Therefore, I never really considered that as a threat because he only saw her that one time.

Being a daughter of pastors, I was taught that sex was only for marriage and to wait until then. I was raised in a God-fearing home, but I was in love with Luke, and I was ready to go deeper in our relationship. We had

How It All Started

already made plans to get married after college, so we figured it wouldn't hurt to start having sex a little early. I didn't think anything was wrong with that. But I was dead wrong. Luke and I always kissed and touched, but we never went all the way. Over summer break, I told him I was determined to do it before our senior year was over, and I guess he was too.

As we walked into his house, I could hear music playing from a distance, and I immediately asked, "Who's here?" in a frantic and confused tone. Luke laughed, amused at me being afraid. "No one is home; all of this is for you." Luke smiled and led me to his bedroom, where the music was coming from. He began to kiss my lips, and then slowly traced my neck with his pillow soft lips; he was so enticing. He began taking my clothes off and caressing every part of my body. Before I knew it, we were on his bed, still kissing. It was like a movie scene, hot and steamy. He began taking his shirt off to reveal that rock-hard six pack, and yes, I rubbed every part of his body too!

As we got under the cover, I remember him asking me "Are you sure?" and I said in a whisper filled with passion, "*Yes!*" Luke immediately began to passionately kiss me, as if he was waiting for this moment for a long time. Luke was so good I couldn't believe he was mine. I know it's strange talking about this because at the time I was still in high school, but it was my senior year, and I was about to be an adult soon. After our little rendezvous, we got dressed and went to school, we missed half of our first period class, but we came up with a pretty good lie, so they didn't notify our parents. I couldn't stop thinking about what happened that morning.

When I got to my second period class, and the teacher split us into groups of three. I was with a guy that I've known since my junior year. We had a few classes together, so we knew each other. Stacy was grouped with us, and they noticed something that I had not. I had a huge hickey on my neck! They laughed and joked about me, and Luke and I couldn't help but laugh with them. But I wasn't prepared for what was in store for me when I got home. As the school day went on, it finally set in that it was almost time to go home, and I thought about my parents and *the hickey*!

I felt a huge knot in my throat because I knew my parents would be upset when they saw it. As I said before, my parents are pastors, and they don't believe in sex before marriage. They taught me that sex was sacred and only for marriage; that's why I valued being celibate. I wanted to wait until marriage, I really did, but Luke made it so hard, and I knew that one day we would get married. Once the final bell rung, I headed to Luke's car, and he drove me home. My mom was a stay-at-home mom, so she was there in the kitchen, cooking dinner.

When I got inside, I yelled from the front door to let my mom know I was home and that I was going to take a shower and do my homework. I figured that would take her focus off coming to talk to me for a little while. Every day, after school my mom and I would talk about how our day went, and I loved that because it made us really close. But this day, I didn't want her to come because I needed to figure out how to hide that big hickey. As I got into the shower, I began washing my body, and I noticed that I had a hickey on my breast. As I washed my body more, I noticed another hickey on my other breast, then another on my stomach, and another one on my neck—I was shocked. I didn't realize Luke was all over me like that! I was engrossed in the sex to realize he left hickeys all over my body. I had a total of five hickeys on my body, two on my neck, two on my breast, and one on my stomach. I was mortified of the thought of my parents finding out about these hickeys.

The Strawberry Seeds

As I finished washing up, I hurried to get my makeup from the cabinet and ran to my room. I was rushing to lotion my body when suddenly I heard a knock on the door. My eyes were locked on the door, and my head was filled with crazy thoughts; I did not want to answer the door. "Who is it?" I asked. "It's me, your mom. I just wanted to come talk to you about something." I didn't know what to do next; my mind was so busy running, I just wrapped the towel around and opened the door. Boy, did I regret that! My mom came and started telling me about plans that she and my dad had that weekend, when she abruptly stopped and stared in disbelief at me. I could feel the biggest knot in my stomach and in my throat at the same time.

"What is that on your neck?" my mom asked.

I said "What?" That was the dumbest thing I could have said to my mom at that moment because I could see her eyes began to fill with rage after I said that.

"Don't play dumb with me; what is that on your neck? You have two hickeys on your neck! What have you been doing? When did you get this? Where have you been? So you and Luke are having sex now?"

All I could hear was my mom yelling at the top of her lungs, asking question after question about me and Luke

How It All Started

having sex. I didn't get a chance to answer the questions because she was so busy yelling and asking. My mind was blank at that moment because I knew I had messed up; I knew it was wrong.

"So you think it's okay to have hickeys all over your neck like that? You know guys will think you're a ho now? Is that what you want people to think of you? I can't believe you! I'm so disappointed in you!"

My mom left the room and slammed the door extra hard. I guess she wanted to make sure I knew she was upset. I couldn't do anything but cry; I was hurt and in disbelief because my mom had basically said I was a ho because I had hickeys all over my body. I was hurt and disappointed in my mother because I didn't expect her to react like that. I knew she would be pissed but not to the point of calling me a name like that. My mind was racing, my heart was aching, and all I wanted to do was go to sleep. I didn't even want to come out my room for dinner, but I went to eat, and not a word was said at the table. My dad was out late still working, so it was just me and my mom.

After dinner, she went to her room and got on the phone with one of my aunts. I could hear her telling my aunt the whole thing, and I was infuriated. I felt betrayed by my mom. I guess I had said more than I realized to her during the argument because she told my aunt that I said I went to Luke house before school and that we had sex there. I didn't remember saying anything to her, but I guess I don't remember because my mind was so blank from all her yelling at the time. I was hurt that my mom was basically gossiping about me over the phone, and it hurt because I didn't want my business out there. I didn't want my extended family knowing any of this.

I did my homework and went to bed that evening. I was too upset to even talk to Luke that night. My mom didn't want me riding with Luke anymore; she made me start riding the bus again. I hated the bus, but I understood her reasoning of not trusting me and Luke anymore. Luke and I would still meet up at school and would ride to his place for a quick sex session before first period. Luke lived near our school, so it worked out perfectly. We did this at least three times out of the week.

I enjoyed the thrill of it all, but one day we had just finished having sex, and we realized that we had missed the whole first-period class. We frantically got dressed and got in his car to head back to school, but as Luke was pulling out the driveway, he didn't realize that his car door was still open, and it hit the garage door. The impact made his car door bend backward and caused a huge dint. The garage door wouldn't close at first, so he had to fix the door somehow to get it to close. My heart was racing because I just knew that somehow his parents were going to find out and then tell my parents. I was so afraid that all I could do was just pray. I know that sounds crazy. I was just sinning with Luke and knowing I was praying to not get exposed. I deserved every bit of being exposed, but somehow Luke got the garage door closed, and we headed back to school.

The school ended up calling my mom, but I told her my teacher must have did the attendance check when I went to the restroom. After that experience, I felt as if that was God warning me to stop having sex in the morning before school, and I did. I told Luke that we couldn't do that anymore because it was too much of a risk, so he agreed, but we still found ways to have sex after school. I knew sex was a sin and that God wasn't pleased, but I guess lust had a hold on me.

As months passed, we started getting closer to prom and graduation. Prom came up first, and I had the time of my life. My parents took me to get my makeup done by a MAC makeup artist, and my face was beautiful! I had a mermaid-style dress, strapless gown with sequins and glitter all over. It was a beautiful maroon color, and I felt like I was going to be the belle of the ball.

I was exhilarated for Luke to pick me up. We went to have dinner at a restaurant with all of our friends and then hit the road on a party bus to the prom. It was a memorable night to say the least, and after we left prom, Luke and I went to have some alone time before he took me back home. We went to have sex in his car in an empty mall parking lot. We were risk-takers, and I loved it.

Graduation finally came, and we were thrilled. My family came from out of town, and Stacy, Kaley, and I had a big graduation party together. It was the best way to end our senior year together. After that, Kaley got accepted to a college in Europe, where she always said she wanted to go, and Stacy got accepted to a college in Florida. It was a big move for them because we were all born and raised in Texas. Luke and I were going to a college right in Texas, and it was only forty-five minutes from where we lived. It was perfect because it was a Christian university, and that was something that I valued.

Chapter 2

A Plus One or Two

That summer after graduation was the best summer we had together. Kaley, Stacy, and I went to Jamaica as a graduation gift from our parents. We had such a good time; we stayed at a resort for an entire week, and it was all-inclusive. We ate and drank and enjoyed ourselves. We met a couple of sexy guys, Liam, Larry, and Lance. They were brothers, from America as well; they were there celebrating their birthdays. We went to explore the tourist attractions with these guys. The funny thing is that they were twenty-four-year-old fraternal triplets, and we could tell them apart. We had a great time with them, they invited us to drink and play games in their room, and of course, we went. We had so much fun.

The Strawberry Seeds

I know I shouldn't have been there, knowing that I was in a relationship, but I had just graduated. I wanted to live life. What Luke didn't know wasn't going to hurt him, or so I thought. I had my eyes on the oldest triplet, Liam, who had green eyes with blonde hair and the chiseled features of a sports model, and his body was perfect too. I couldn't help but smile every time he would come around. He would always sit next to me on the tourist rides. I could definitely feel the sexual tension between us.

That night they invited us to their room, where we played cards and drank until two in the morning. Liam finally asked me if I wanted to go for a walk along the beach, and of course, I said yes. We walked along the ocean, talking about everything from our desires in life, to our families, and he even told me that he was a firefighter from Texas. He lived thirty minutes from where my parents lived. What a small world. We learned a lot about each other on that walk. Finally we started getting tired, so we headed back to my room.

When we finally got to my room, I opened my room door, and as he turned to walk away, I grabbed his arm to pull him in for a kiss. That kiss was filled with passion, desire, and lust; I couldn't help myself and, apparently, neither could he. As we kissed, we started making steps toward the bed and one-by-one, pieces of clothing began to hit the floor. Before we knew it, we were in the bed, completely naked. My phone started ringing, which is what woke us up that morning, and it was Luke calling. I was too ashamed to answer, so I just ignored the call. I didn't want to think about him at that moment, and I definitely didn't want to tell him what happened yet. I loved Luke, and I knew I had messed up big time, but for some reason it didn't stop me from doing it again.

From that night on, Liam and I would find an excuse to get away from the group to have sex and spend time together. Our trip finally came to an end, and I was sad to go. I had had the time of my life with my girls and with Liam. Liam asked to exchange numbers so we could stay in touch and maybe link up back home in Dallas. When I got back home, I was happy to greet my mom and dad at the airport. They asked about the trip, and I told them everything—well, except all the sex with Liam. They were delighted to know that we had a great time. The ride home was relaxing, but I wasn't ready for what was waiting for me at home.

The Strawberry Seeds

When we pulled into our driveway, I noticed Luke's car in the driveway, and that's when guilt hit me like a ton of bricks. I felt butterflies in my stomach. I just wanted to run away, but I couldn't. I wasn't ready to see Luke so soon; I wanted to at least give it a couple of days to let my mind settle. When I got inside of the house, I saw Luke sitting on the couch with the biggest smile ever, and I couldn't help but feel more guilt all over again. He hugged me really tight and told me he had a big surprise for me. So he lead me out to the backyard of my parents' house, and as I looked out, my eyes began to fill with tears.

He had helped my dad build a beautiful firepit in the backyard, and he had a whole setup for me and him to do smores and watch movies back there. I was so shocked I couldn't do anything but cry because I was so guilty and wrong. I didn't deserve this guy at all; he was thrilled to do this for me while I was away enjoying another guy.

"Baby, what's wrong? I was hoping you would like it," he said in a concerned tone.

"Yes, I love it. I wasn't expecting it at all!" I said as he came and hugged me with a tight embrace. I knew I had to tell him the truth but I didn't want to ruin our moment, so I waited. We watched movies and ate smores until it

A Plus One or Two

was time for him to go home. I knew I had to tell him, and I had to tell him soon.

Liam finally texted me when he got back from Jamaica, and he wanted to meet up on one of his days off. I was so excited that I told him yes. I know what you're thinking, but I just couldn't help myself. Liam and Luke were totally different, but I liked both. They didn't know about each other either. Let's just say Liam was my sneaky link. Luke wanted to take me on a date to the Great Wolf Lodge a week after I got back from Jamaica, and it was fun. We stayed there the entire weekend, and we had a great time. I still wasn't ready to tell him about Liam, so I just continued to push it back to a later date. Every time I felt like I wanted to tell him, something would get in the way.

I was also seeing Liam on his days off, and I would stay the night at Liam's apartment, as he lived alone. My parents thought that I was always with Kaley and Stacy; well, that's what I had them thinking. I told my parents that I wanted to enjoy them before they left for school, but I was actually either with Liam or Luke. Summer was getting close to an end, and I was excited about getting ready to go to a university. I had an app on my phone that kept track of my periods, and it was pretty accurate about my period. But my tracker notified me that I was two weeks past due, and I didn't even realize it. I was so busy enjoying my summer with Liam and Luke that I forgot about everything else.

The crazy thing is that I didn't use protection with Luke because we felt like we were going to be get married anyway, and he would always pull out. Liam and I used protection a couple of times, and then we stopped because we felt comfortable with each other. I know that's crazy, but I was young and stupid. I could have caught anything, but I know God was watching over me, even in my dumb choices. When I realized that I had missed a period, I went to the store to get a pregnancy test and took it right at the store in the restroom. I remember when I saw the results; my eyes were huge and filled with tears, and my heart began to race. All I could do was just stare in disbelief; my body was frozen in place and my mind was too. My phone took me out of shock when it started ringing, and when I went to see who it was, the test fell to the floor.

I looked at my phone and realized that it was my mom, so I answered. She called to tell me about a revival that they were having at the church, and she really wanted me to be there that night, so I told her yes without hesitating.

A Plus One or Two

I knew I needed some Jesus after seeing that pregnancy test. After I got off the phone, I headed to lunch with Kaley and Stacy. This was our last get-together before they were leaving off to school, and I had to tell them the news. When we got to the restaurant, we talked and laughed like our usual selves, but strangely, Stacy knew something was wrong with me.

Finally, I burst into tears and told them *everything*. I told them that I was still messing around with Liam while Luke and I were together. I gave them every juicy detail, and I felt so much better letting it out too. The beautiful thing about Kaley and Stacy is that they never judged me; they always loved me no matter what crazy things I did. But as friends, they did tell me the truth even when it hurt. And that's what they told me on that day, that I had to tell the truth to Liam and Luke. I hated how that sounded, but I knew I had to do it.

After that fun and relaxing outing with the girls, I had to head home and get ready for my parents' church revival. I rode with my mom and dad to church, and I was feeling down the whole way there. I didn't think my parents had noticed my mood, but they did. When we got to church, my mom pulled me into her office and asked me what was wrong. I told my mom that I was fine, but she knew I was lying, so she just told me to come to her when I felt ready to talk. I was afraid to tell my mom because of what happened with the hickey situation the year before. I didn't want to be judged again.

Finally, the revival got started; the praise and worship team was singing, and I began worshiping. Before I knew it, God had come in, and all I could do was just praise and worship Him. Then the pastor, who was supposed to preach, came up to me and ministered to me. He said, "God said this is His doing, trust Him, and you are going to make it out. God loves you so much and through this, He is causing you to come closer to Him. God said don't worry; I got you and your child." When he said that last part, I instantly started crying and praising God, because God still loved me after all that I had done.

My dirt was dirty, it was worst than dirty, yet God took the time to tell me He loves me. I was extremely grateful. The pastor began to pray over me, and then he had my parents to hold me as he ministered to them. He told my parents to not judge me but to be there for me and that God was going to use me in a mighty way. He told them that people needed to hear my voice. After he got done ministering to us, he prayed over us, and then the night continued with a blessed word, dinner with the guest pastors, and then home.

As I began to get ready for bed, my mom came into my room. She apologized for the argument about the hickey and expressed to me how proud she is of me and how much she loves me. She told me a lot that night, and that's when I told her that I was pregnant. She cried when I told her, but it wasn't a sad cry; it was tears of joy. She was ecstatic to hear that she was going to be a grandmother; she didn't judge me at all—instead, she showered me with love. She told me that she and my dad would have my back through it all. I was thrilled and relieved to hear that, and all I could do was just cry. She embraced me with a hug full of love and compassion. I knew that God was with me and this baby.

I was ready to tell Luke the truth, and I was ready to tell Liam the truth as well. I signed up for the community college near my parents' house, and I even found a job at a daycare as well. I had made up in my mind that I was going to take care of myself and this baby, no matter what Luke or Liam might do. I didn't know which of them was the father, so I didn't expect them to stay by my side during the pregnancy. I decided to tell Luke first because he was my boyfriend, and it was only right for me to. I told him I wanted to do a movie night around my parents' firepit in the backyard. He came over on a Friday night, and we laughed, talked, and ate smores. Finally, I told him everything from the night with Liam until finding out I was pregnant.

I could tell he was devastated; he was silent for what seemed like ten minutes. He told me he needed time to think and that he didn't want to hear from me unless it was about the baby. He said we weren't together anymore until he decided on what he really wanted, but he would still be there for the baby. So basically, he broke up with me. I had prepared myself for that, but I was hurting because I knew I had hurt Luke. I didn't mean to do that to him because he was perfectly good to me.

Finally, I went to Liam's place and told him everything. Liam was upset at the fact that I never told him that I was in a relationship, but he said that he would want to be with me if I wasn't with Luke anymore. I was surprised to get that response from Liam, but he really expressed to me how much he really liked me. I told Liam that I wanted to take things slow because I didn't know what I really wanted.

Chapter 3

Undeserving

I started going to a community college near my parents' house. I studied general studies because I was still unsure on my major. Luke started school at the university where we were supposed to go to together. He would call to check on my doctor appointments, but he didn't want to talk about anything else besides the baby. I was hurt, but I understood that Luke needed his space, and he was more hurt than me.

My relationship with Liam began to develop even more, and I started getting stronger feelings for him. He started sending money for me to put in savings for things the baby needed. He would always call just to check on my well-being, and I loved that. He was concerned about me and the baby, and that was what made me like him even more. Since Liam and I started getting closer, I decided it was time for him to meet my parents. I invited him over for dinner with me and my parents, and yes, I cooked. I made chicken alfredo with spinach, a side salad, and garlic rolls. I felt so good but nervous as to how everything would turn out. The night went well; my parents really liked him, and he really liked my parents.

Liam invited me out on a double date with his parents, and I was nervous to see how they would react to me being a black girl. I was so happy to meet his parents, and I was even happier to see that they accepted me just the way I was. What's funny is that Liam's parents were pastors as well, and they had a new ministry. They were excited about meeting my parents and fellowshipping together. I felt like my life was perfect at that moment because everything was coming together so smoothly. Oh, I forgot, we did tell his parents about the pregnancy and that the baby could potentially be his, and they still accepted me.

I loved Luke, but his parents were not supportive of me being pregnant. The crazy thing is that they didn't even know that the baby could potentially not be his. They didn't want Luke to settle down or have children until after he graduated from college. His parents were very strict about that. I was hurt at how unsupportive they were. They even said that I should think about abortion. They said that they were concerned for Luke's future. I knew I wasn't going to have an abortion because I knew that it was wrong. God created life, and I was not going to destroy it because someone else doesn't think it's the right time.

All of that caused a distance between Luke and me, as well as the fact that I had cheated on him. Luke finally told me that he forgave me and that we could be friends, but he wanted to focus on his education. So we only talked when I had updates about the baby. Thus, when Liam's family accepted me, I was thrilled to have him as a part of my life. The fact that his family was a God-fearing family, like mine, was a huge plus for me. I finally told Liam that I was ready to be in a relationship, and he was excited about that. He came to the majority of my doctor visits; if he couldn't come, it was because he was working.

Liam loved being a firefighter, but I was afraid that something might happen to him. College was going well, my relationship with Liam and his family was going perfect, and I even started getting more involved in my parents' ministry. I started helping in the children ministry, and I enjoyed it. As the months passed, I started showing more, and it was interesting to see my belly grow. I was embracing this pregnancy as much as I could, and I wasn't going to let anyone make me feel bad. As we got into the winter months, closer to my due date, my mom and Liam's mom decided to throw me a baby shower, and it was beautiful. I enjoyed it; they even invited Luke and his family, but only Luke showed up. They did the gender reveal at the baby shower, and it turned out I was having a baby girl. It's funny because me and Luke always talked about if we had a boy, we would name him Luk-a because Luke plus Mia equals Luka, but we never had a girl name.

Liam always said if he had a girl, he would like the name Leah. I was exhilarated that I was going to be having a mini-me. Kaley and Stacy were excited too. My mom surprised me with them coming, by doing the baby shower around their winter break. Kaley, Stacy, and I spent a lot of time together before it was time for them to head back to their schools. They were thrilled; they wanted my baby to call them aunt. I didn't object because they were like sisters to me.

As time passed, it got closer to my due date, and I was getting nervous. The thought of me becoming a mom at the age of eighteen was scary for me. I was praying that I would become a great mother. I wanted to teach my daughter about God. The week before my due date Liam proposed to me. He took me to a fancy restaurant and made it a beautiful night, especially for me. He told me that he wanted to spend the rest of his life with me. He said that even if the baby wasn't his, he would be her father and take care of us both for the rest of his life because he loved us.

Hearing Liam say those words just blessed my soul! I felt like I wanted to jump on top of him right at that moment. Liam was perfect at making me feel special, and that's what I loved about him. He accepted me, flaws and all. So I told him yes—yes, to being his wife, yes to being his forever, and yes to having his last name. Liam's last name was Hanes, and I couldn't help but rehearse saying Mia Hanes over and over. I showed my parents the beautiful engagement ring. It was stunning; he had to have spent a nice amount on it. My parents knew that he was proposing to me because he had asked them after the baby shower, and of course, they said yes.

The Strawberry Seeds

My parents were becoming great friends with his parents, and they even began ministering at each other's churches. I was overjoyed how my life was turning out, but deep down inside I kept feeling like I didn't deserve all the love I was getting. I felt like I was horrible for how I treated Luke. I did Luke wrong, and now I was happy with the guy I cheated on Luke with. I knew Luke was hurt when he found out that Liam and I were getting married, and it crushed me. That was something Luke and I would talk about all the time throughout high school. We talked about how we were going to go to college together, graduate, get our dream jobs, get married, and have a beautiful family.

The night after the proposal I started getting some serious pain in my abdomen. It was like a tightening pain that radiated through my back and my stomach. At first, I tried to ignore the pain, but as the night went on, it got worst. Hour by hour, the pain got more intense until I couldn't take it anymore. My mom took me to the hospital, and she called my dad and Liam to meet us up there. When we got to the hospital, I was checked to see if I was dilated. I was six centimeters, so the doctor admitted me and took me to my room.

It didn't take long for Liam to get to the hospital. I was in excruciating pain; the doctor had to break my water because my water bag didn't break on its own. I was trying to handle the pain as my mom sat there trying to coach me through. Liam didn't know what to do, so he just held my hand during each contraction. It was comforting having Liam there holding my hand. Finally, hours later it was time to push, and it literally took thirty minutes to get that baby girl out. When I heard that beautiful cry, I was filled with joy. They placed her on my chest, and all I could do was cry.

I was finally face-to-face with my baby girl, and I knew instantly that I wanted her name to be Leah. Leah Hanes was her name, and I didn't have a doubt that she wasn't Liam's because she looked just like him. She was striking with almond-shaped green eyes, blonde straight hair, and full lips. She was our angel sent from above. At that moment, I knew it was meant for me and Liam to be together. Liam was overjoyed to see her as well; all he could do was cry, and of course, he wanted to hold her. I was on cloud nine, God had given me two additions. He had given me Liam, and he gave me our beautiful daughter, Leah, and that was my plus two.

The Strawberry Seeds

I finally called Luke to tell him that I had Leah, and he came to visit once I got home from the hospital. Luke didn't seem interested in visiting, but he finally came, and when he did, I think he realized that Leah wasn't his. I think he had a feeling all along that she wasn't going to be his, but he still tagged along this crazy ride with us. I was happy to see Luke when he came to visit me and Leah at my parents' house. He held her for the first time, and all he could do was just stare at her. "You are beautiful, just like your mommy," Luke said to Leah in a low tone. I was not expecting to hear those words come out of his mouth, especially seeing that she looked more like Liam then me.

It gave me butterflies hearing Luke talk to Leah in such a loving way. It made me think of the Luke that I fell in love with and the Luke that I gave my virginity to. He held her until she went to sleep in his arms, and then he left. Liam and Luke did the paternity test and had gotten the results. We officially found out that Liam was the father of Leah, and he was head over heels about it. I didn't hear anything from Luke after that. I always prayed the best for Luke because I still loved him, and I wanted him to be happy.

UNDESERVING

Liam and I wanted to get married right away so we could move in together. We didn't want to move in together without being married because we just didn't feel right doing that. So we got married when Leah was about three months old. It was a small wedding with just our parents, his brothers, and of course, Kaley and Stacy were able to attend as well. I couldn't believe that just a year before I was graduating from high school, and here I am, a mother to a beautiful baby girl and getting married. Yes, getting married to the man I never saw coming. I felt undeserving of all this love. I was dirty for hurting Luke and causing him so much pain. I was dirty for lying and cheating. I was dirty for having sex out of wedlock. I was dirty for sleeping with two guys at the same time. I was dirty, yet all these people were showing me love. I felt so undeserving.

Chapter 4

Devastation

Leah and I moved into Liam's apartment, and I was thrilled because this was my first time moving out of my parents' house. His apartment was really nice, with granite countertops in the kitchen and the bathrooms. Our apartment was in a beautifully developed area with ample restaurants and stores. Liam invited me to his fire station and even gave me a tour of their kitchen and sleeping quarters. I met his fellow firefighters, and I started feeling like a real wife at that moment. I couldn't believe I was only eighteen, married to a twenty-four-year-old, and living life happily. We had a six-year age difference, but it didn't feel like it because I was mature for my age. I enjoyed staying at home caring for Leah, and on the days that I had school, my mom or Mrs. Hanes (Liam's mom) would babysit Leah. I loved having the support.

Mrs. Hanes was such a blessing to me in so many ways because she treated me like I was her very own daughter. Mrs. Hanes had always wanted a daughter, but after she had the triplets, she didn't want to have any more children. I don't blame her because that's a lot of skin stretching and risk taking. Some days when I didn't have class, I would go over to Mrs. Hanes's house and just sit and chat with her. She had a lot of wisdom, and I loved that about her. The crazy thing is that I never felt that way around Luke's parents. I just liked them because they seemed to like me, but that was before I got pregnant.

The Hanes didn't care about my past or whether I had a degree or not; they accepted me. Our birthdays came up. Liam's was in June, and he turned twenty-five; and then mine was in August, and I turned nineteen. Time flew, and before I knew it, Leah was crawling, walking, and saying her first words. Her first birthday came and then her second birthday and then our second anniversary. We had planned a cruise to the Bahamas for our second anniversary, and it was a blast. We enjoyed every bit of it; we were on the cruise for seven days as it went from one

The Strawberry Seeds

destination to the next. Liam made me feel very special on this cruise, and I didn't want to go home. The last day of the cruise I remember soaking up those last precious moments with Liam before we headed back to Texas.

When we got home, Leah was so excited to see us that she didn't want her daddy to go back to work. Liam took Leah to get ice cream and gave her some one-on-one time with him. I was happy because it gave me some mommy time. That night, he packed his bag to get ready for his four-day shift at the fire station. The next day, I made him breakfast, and then he went to work. I did my usual errands, I took Leah to the park to play, and then we went home to make dinner. I gave Leah a bath and then did my usual praying and reading before I went to bed. I was fast asleep when I began to have disturbing dreams, and I would wake up without remembering what was going on in the dream. I just remember the dreams were bad, and they caused me to toss and turn through the night until my phone rang at three o'clock in the morning. I was startled by my phone because of it ringing that time of morning.

I had a bad feeling before I even picked the phone up, and my throat felt tight like a huge lump was in it. I could feel my heart beginning to beat faster, and then

DEVASTATION

I answered. "Hello....Yes, this is Mrs. Hanes...What!" I dropped the phone in disbelief of the news that I had just received. My husband was severely injured and in surgery. I rushed and got my clothes on, I called my mom, my in-laws, and rushed to the hospital with Leah.

When I got to the hospital, I asked about my husband, and the nurses told me that he was still in surgery. I wanted more information, but they wouldn't give me any at the moment. A little after I arrived, Mr. and Mrs. Hanes arrived, and my parents did too. My mom tried to comfort me, while my dad took Leah and rocked her back to sleep. Mr. and Mrs. Hanes were trying to stay strong, and my mom could tell, so she said, "Let's pray because God is in control." When she said that, we all came together and began praying for Liam, my love. After my mom had finished praying, the doctor came to speak to us, and that's when we found out. *My husband was dead.*

The room went silent, my mind went blank, and it felt as if my lungs were closing in. It felt like I couldn't breathe, like I was gasping for air. I was having a panic attack. I couldn't believe it; as a matter of fact, I didn't want to believe it! I couldn't do anything but scream and cry and scream and cry. My mom and Mrs. Hanes came to comfort me, but I could tell they were hurting too. I wanted to be strong for Mrs. Hanes because her child was gone. I couldn't even imagine what it would feel like to lose a child.

We hugged and cried together while my mom prayed. It felt like we were like this for hours, but it was only a few minutes when the surgeon asked if we wanted to view his body. Mrs. Hanes and I went together, and it was not a pleasant sight to see. He was burnt beyond what I imagined when I had gotten the call from the hospital. He didn't even look like himself. My hurt was filled with pain, suffering, devastation, denial, and guilt. I was angry, and the one I was angry at was God. I didn't understand why this horrible thing had to happen to Liam. Why did he have to suffer like this; why did he have to leave so soon?

I should have been the one who was dead. I began to wonder whether this was my punishment for treating Luke the way I did. Was this my punishment for cheating and lying? Was I being punished? I asked God so many questions because I was terribly confused and hurt. I stopped going to church, I quit school, and I even quit being a mom. My parents took Leah for a while because they knew what I was going through, and they didn't want Leah seeing her mommy like that. I didn't eat for days, I

DEVASTATION

couldn't sleep, and I was depressed. I was depressed to the point of contemplating suicide.

My love was gone; the man that I was planning on having more children with was gone. The man that I was just enjoying the beautiful cruise with was gone. I kept replaying those precious moments we had together, and it caused my heart to ache even more. Liam was twenty-seven when he died. I was planning on going to Vegas for his twenty-eighth birthday, and then he died. I didn't even get to tell him goodbye. He risked his life saving someone else's life, and I loved that about him when he was alive. Liam was such a caring person; he would put others before himself. He was definitely a servant leader because he served people, and he loved doing it. Liam was a great man of faith, and he made sure that we prayed as a family. We did daily devotionals together because he wanted us to stay connected with God. Liam was a strong man of God, and he was gone just like that.

I was in a depression for months, and I didn't even notice. Mrs. Hanes would come over to check on me, but she couldn't help me. No one could help me; I was damaged. I pulled myself away from everyone because I just wanted to be alone. I even stopped seeing Leah because she reminded me so much of Liam, especially because she looked just like him. My birthday came up in August, and I didn't even realize it until my mom called to wish me a happy birthday. It was my birthday, and I was not even interested in celebrating. I was supposed to be celebrating this day with my love, and he was gone forever.

Kaley and Stacy tried to call to comfort me, but I even pushed them away. I pushed everyone that I loved away. I was at a breaking point; I was on the verge of just ending my life, when one day, out of nowhere, I got a phone call. My phone rang and rang and rang. I didn't want to answer, but this person was persistent, so I finally gave in and answered.

Chapter 5

Switching Sides (Luke)—Part One

I went through a lot those four years of high school. I was with Avery a year before I met Mia. I remember the day I laid eyes on Mia Hawthorne in study hall. She was sexy, and I had to get her number. I know I was a flirt, but I was always faithful to Avery and never cheated on her. As Mia and I started getting closer as friends, I noticed that she was becoming distant. It started to get more distant between us, and that's when she decided to talk to an upperclassman. I didn't know until she called me one day. Avery told me that she cheated on me with an upperclassman, not only once, but multiple times. That's when I decided to end it. I didn't want to jump into a relationship right away after that, because Avery really hurt me.

I really liked Mia, but I didn't want to jump into a relationship with her because I valued her as a friend, and I didn't want to mess that up. Mia and I would talk about everything, so I really liked her, and I didn't want her to be my rebound. That summer, I got a job at the mall, and that's when I met Ashley. Ashley was really hot, and she would always flirt with me during work. Ashley and I worked a lot of shifts together, so I started to like her, but only in a sexual way. I didn't want a relationship because I knew Ashley just wanted a fling. She didn't want a relationship, and neither did I. One evening when we were closing the store together, Ashley invited me over to her place to play video games. Ashley's parents weren't home, so I knew instantly this wasn't a game night but, instead, a fun night. Ashley led me through a dark house to her bedroom, which was big. She began kissing me and then taking off my clothes; one thing led to another, and let's just say it became an interesting night. After that, I went home, and as I lay in bed, I began to feel like I had finally gotten over Avery.

Switching Sides (Luke)—Part One

Ashley and I became friends with benefits, which worked out great for both of us. I still was getting closer to Mia over the summer, and that's when it finally hit me that I wanted to be in a relationship with Mia. So when summer came to an end, I finally asked Mia to be my girl, and she said yes. I was excited to have her because I knew I could trust her. I stopped working at the mall when I started my sophomore year, but I still stayed in contact with Ashley. Ashley was my good friend (if you know what I mean), so I couldn't let go of that, especially because I wasn't getting anything from Mia. Mia always talked about how she was a Christian and she wanted to wait until marriage. I played along with Mia and told her that I would wait for marriage, but I was still seeing Ashley. I knew I was wrong for that, especially because Avery had cheated on me, but I was at a point of not caring anymore. I felt like I couldn't trust females, but deep down inside, I wanted to make myself trust again.

Ashley was great in bed compared to Avery, and I liked that about her. Avery was my first, but she was boring with sex. Ashley was exciting because she always wanted to try something new, and I liked that about her. As time went on, I began to develop stronger feelings for Mia, and I finally decided to end things with Ashley. Ashley told me to keep her number just in case I needed it again, and I kept it. Mia and I started talking about college and how we wanted to go to the same university. We talked about getting an apartment together and then eventually graduating and getting married.

My feelings became stronger for Mia, and she was finally ready to go to the next level with me. It was the summer before our senior year when Mia started saying she was ready to lose her virginity. I was excited to hear that, so I started planning. I wanted our first time to be a time to remember, so I made it our first day of school senior year. I made sure my parents were gone to work, and my sister rode to school with her friends. I had the house to myself, so I began setting up my room. I tried to set the mood by putting rose petals on the bed and then I turned on some old-school love songs in my room. I picked Mia up, and I began driving as if we were headed to school, but then I turned and headed to my house. I could see the puzzled look on her face; she was confused. Once we got to my place, I took her into my house, and I could tell she was nervous, but I reassured her that everything was fine. I wanted her to feel as comfortable

SWITCHING SIDES (LUKE)—PART ONE

as possible, and I guess she did because we got down to business quickly.

After that day, we were inseparable; we wanted each other all the time. Her mom didn't want me picking her up for school anymore once she found out, so we started meeting at school, and we would leave first period to have sex. Ashley and I texted from time to time just to check on each other, but I didn't want it to go any further than just friendly conversation. I loved Mia, and I didn't want to mess that up. I knew eventually I would have to tell her the truth about the beginning of our relationship. I knew I had to tell her that I was cheating on her with Ashley the first year of our relationship, but I wasn't ready. Mia was under the impression that I only had sex with Ashley once because I couldn't get up the nerve to tell her the truth. Our senior year went by too fast. I couldn't believe I was about to be in college.

Mia's parents sent her and her friends to Jamaica for her graduation gift, and I missed her a lot. I spent that time helping Mia's dad, Mr. Hawthorne, build a firepit in their backyard. I enjoyed Mia's parents, and I felt like I could be myself around them. They accepted me and treated me like I was their son. My parents were more uptight and conservative. I felt like a misfit in my family because I wasn't like them. My sister was more like my parents, so she was looked at as the "golden child." The fact that I was dating Mia made it worse because my parents wanted me to date a girl with parents who had more money. My parents have their own law firm, and they have wealthy clients, so they are pretty well known.

My parents felt like Mia didn't fit in, but Mia didn't know that. I made Mia believe that my parents were crazy about her, and my parents pretended with her as well. I just didn't want Mia to dislike me because of my parents, so I made her think they really liked her. Once Mia got back from her trip, things were back to the same, and we were preparing for college. We spent the summer over at each other's places and hanging out when she wasn't with Kaley and Stacy. One night, Mia invited me over to watch movies and chill, or so I thought, but she ended up telling me that she met a guy in Jamaica.

She said that she had been cheating and then it continued once she got back home. The guy lived in Texas as well, but the crazy thing is that she continued things with him while we were together. I know I did dirt, but I never thought that Mia would do something like this; it caught

SWITCHING SIDES (LUKE)—PART ONE

me off guard. The worst part was when she said she was pregnant, and she didn't know if it was mine or his. That hurt me to the core, my girl cheated and may be pregnant with another dude's baby. I told her that I needed space and left immediately. Just in case the baby was mine, I wanted to know how the baby was developing, so I would call to check on the progress of the baby. After every doctor appointment, Mia would call to tell me about the baby. I loved hearing her talk about the baby, but it would hurt every time I thought about it potentially not being mine.

I told my parents about Mia being pregnant because they asked why she wasn't going to the university anymore. My parents were upset; they wanted Mia to have an abortion, but I never told them that it may not be mine. My parents didn't want me to have a baby because they wanted me to finish school, get my career established, and then get married. I didn't mind starting a family with Mia before all of that because I loved Mia, but after she hurt me like that, I was done with her. I started college, and I and my dorm mate, Aaron, became good friends. Aaron was studying to become a doctor like me. We went to every party, and we talked to every hot girl we came across. I wanted Mia far from my mind because I was hurt.

Chapter 6

Switching Sides (Luke)—Part Two

College was going great. I was making more friends, and I finally crossed paths with Ashley again. She was going to the same college as me, and we happened to have our English class together. We hung out all the time, and we even decided to become friends with benefits again. Everything was going well, and the first semester was coming to an end when I got a call from Mia's mom, inviting me to the baby shower. I wasn't going to go, but I finally got the courage to go. Just in case the baby was mine, I wanted to be there for it. So I went to the baby

Switching Sides (Luke)—Part Two

shower to find out that she was in a relationship with the guy that she cheated on me with.

I was hurt all over again, but this time rage overtook me, and I decided to leave early. That was something Mia and I talked about for years, and she's experiencing it with another guy. I never wanted to see Mia again after that, but I knew I had to deal with the issue of the baby potentially being mine. I didn't call Mia as much because I didn't want to hear her sweet voice. I began getting closer to Ashley and confiding in her, and she understood me. Eventually, Ashley and I decided to make our relationship official, and before I knew it, I got the call that Mia had the baby. I didn't want to go yet, but Ashley talked me into going. So I went, and when I got to the Hawthorne's house, I was nervous to see what this bundle of joy would look like.

When I went inside, Mia came to the living room holding a tiny baby girl, and she asked, "Do you want to hold her?" I shook my head yes immediately. I was eager to see what she looked like, and just as Mia was handing her to me, she said, "Her name is Leah," and I locked eyes with Leah. I knew immediately that Leah wasn't mine because she looked like the guy at the baby shower, but she was beautiful, just like her mother. I couldn't help but to say, "You are beautiful, like your mommy," and I meant it. As I held that tiny precious baby in my arms, all I began to think about was all the conversations we had about children and names that we liked. I never saw this coming—I never imagined my girl, Mia Hawthorne, having another man's baby. This was supposed to be a moment that Mia and I would share together, but I guess God had another plan.

I was never really religious, my parents didn't go to church, and the only time I went to church was with my grandmother. My grandma would take my sister and me to church every time we would visit her in Florida, and I loved going to church. As I got older, I wasn't really interested in church, but when I started dating Mia, I started going to her parents' church with her. I actually enjoyed going to their church, and I even joined the youth group and started connecting with Christian guys. After Mia and I broke up, I stopped attending church and started drinking and partying more. I lost contact with the guys I met at church, and I had a whole new circle of friends. I felt like this was my punishment from God because I didn't tell Mia that I cheated with Ashley the entire first year of our relationship. I felt like God was punishing me

SWITCHING SIDES (LUKE)—PART TWO

for lying to Mia. As I sat there, looking at Leah, I could feel the pain, hurt, and betrayal beginning to consume my mind, so I handed her back to Mia and left.

As soon as I got in my car, I couldn't control my emotions anymore. Tears began to stream down my face. I had never felt this kind of hurt before, and it wasn't a good feeling. I loved Mia more than I had thought; Mia was my friend before we even started dating, and we became closer when we were together. We told each other everything, and that's what I loved about our relationship. I trusted Mia with everything, and then it all came crashing down. We finally did the paternity test, and the results came back that I was not the father. I knew I wasn't the father, but it hurt even more to actually have it confirmed through a test. Deep down inside, I wanted Leah to be mine, but I knew she wasn't, and that hurt so badly. After that, I completely stopped talking to Mia and focused on my education.

Ashley and I broke up after a year of our relationship because I wasn't ready to fully trust and commit. I didn't trust any female at that point in my life, so I did whatever I wanted to do. It seemed like time was fast-forwarding because before I knew it, I was getting ready to graduate in one more year, with a bachelor's degree, and then head to medical school. I was in class when I got a call from Mrs. Hawthorne telling me that Mia's husband had died and Mia was spiraling down a path of destruction. As she was talking, I began to wonder why she bothered calling me because I didn't care, but then she said, "I know you're probably wondering why am I calling you after all that Mia did to you. But Mia has always loved you, you were her best friend and she told you everything. You and Mia got through everything together, and she trusted you to be there for her no matter what. I know it was God who told me to call you, and I just wanted you to know that God is always in control."

Then, before I knew it, she got off the phone. I was confused as to why she would call me, but I knew she was right: God is in control. The things she said to me stuck in my mind all that day. I still didn't call, because I wasn't over the past. I was in my apartment doing some cleaning when I realized that it was Mia's birthday. When we were together, every year for Mia's birthday I would call her and sing her "Happy Birthday." Lord knows I can't sing, but I didn't care, because it was her birthday and I loved making her feel special. I decided to call her, and I waited

Switching Sides (Luke)—Part Two

for an answer, but she didn't answer, so I tried again. I was determined that I wasn't going to stop until she answered the phone, and finally, she answered. I heard that sweet voice mixed with worry and distress, saying, "Hello?"

That's when I started singing: "Happy birthday to you, happy birthday to you, happy birthday to Mia poo, happy birthday to you!" Before I knew it, she started laughing and then crying hysterically. I didn't know what to do, so I just sat in silence for a while. I just listened to her cry, and it hurt me to hear the hurt in her voice—I just wanted to take it away. Finally, she said, "Thank you, Luke. I thought I would never hear your voice again." I was shocked at what I just heard because she was sincere about it. I never thought that Mia missed me. I thought Mia was happy with that guy and never thought of me again, but I was wrong. Mia thought about me often.

We talked for hours about our lives and what we had been up to. She told me about her marriage and Leah. I found myself comforting her about the death of the guy that took her from me. I realized that the feelings that I had for her never left; they were just dormant. It felt good talking to her that day, and I didn't regret it either, because after that, Mia and I became friends again. I made sure I

The Strawberry Seeds

called to check on her every day, and it felt good to see that she was doing better. We even decided that we wanted to start over with our friendship. We wanted to tell the truth about everything, so I had finally told her about Ashley, and it felt good to finally get that off my chest. I felt like God was giving me another chance with Mia, and I was not going to mess it up.

We started hanging out. She started bringing Leah around me, and I fell in love with Mia all over again. Leah wasn't my biological daughter, but I treated her like she was mine. By the time I finished my senior year of college, I decided that I wanted to make Mia my wife. I didn't know if I was moving too soon, but I wanted to make Mia my woman forever.

Chapter 7

Jumping Ahead (Mia)

That call from Luke saved my life, and I thank God for that. I was going down a spiraling pit into depression, and only God knows if I would have gotten out. I started feeling less alone, and the more I talked to Luke, I stopped drinking and also stopped taking pain pills to help me sleep, and I finally started eating proper meals again. I was glad to have Luke there for me in my darkest moment. We began talking as though we had never stopped; it was like we picked up where we left off. Luke would come to visit me to check on me and Leah.

My parents finally brought Leah back a month after Luke and I started talking. They saw that I was getting back to being myself, so they felt comfortable with Leah coming back home, and honestly, I was glad to have her back. Leah was too small to understand death, so my parents told her that her daddy went to see God, and she accepted that. Leah was going back and forth to my parents' and Liam's parents' houses while I was going through my pain. Once she came back home, we did everything together because I wanted to make sure she didn't feel forgotten. I didn't want Leah to think she wasn't important to me or that I didn't want her anymore, because I did.

As Luke and I became close again, I began to bring Leah around him, and she really liked him. She was always excited about spending time with Luke, and so was I. Luke helped comfort me about Liam's death, and that was exactly what I needed. Luke came to visit us on a weekend, and we had a great time laughing about the old times, and we even talked about our future. We reminisced about how we always said we would get married and have children and work in our professions, but so much had changed. We finally had sex, and it was a magical moment. I hadn't felt Luke's touch in so long that I was craving for more of him. That night was the best night I had had in a long time. I loved Liam, but he never could satisfy me like Luke.

Jumping Ahead (Mia)

Having Luke back this time made me not want to ever let him go. After that night, we decided to date secretly because we weren't ready for people to know, but then suddenly things changed. On the day of Luke's graduation, I had butterflies in my stomach, but I didn't know why. His graduation was such a sight to see. Feelings of joy, anger, happiness, regret, and jealousy began to fill me. I was ecstatic for him, and it filled me with joy to see him reaching his dreams, but I was jealous because my dreams had gone down the drain.

I was angry because I had chosen a different path, and—don't get me wrong—I love my daughter, but I felt like I had nothing because I didn't have my dream. I partially had my dream, which was a child, but I wanted to get a degree, get a good job, get married, buy a big, beautiful home, and then start a family. I had a dream of this perfect life, but at that moment seeing him on that stage made me regret my imperfect life. After the ceremony, we went to dinner with his family, and I tried to mask my frustration, but it was hard. Luke's parents praised him the entire time, and I began to feel inadequate being there with him and his family. There I was, sitting with a group of people who

THE STRAWBERRY SEEDS

looked down on me because I have a daughter, with no job, no degree, and nothing to show of success.

I couldn't take it any longer, so I leaned over to tell Luke that I was leaving. As I leaned over, I saw my parents coming to our table, and my mom had a cute little gift bag that she handed over to Luke as they greeted each other. I figured I could stay a little longer since my family was there, and the atmosphere began to change. I started feeling a peace over me that I had never felt before, and I was back feeling happy and joyous. Finally, we were about to begin eating dessert when Luke stood up at the table. He began with this long love story about us, how we met, how we became friends, how we planned our life together, how we skipped school together, and how we got into the same college, and how we split up. He told everyone how much he loves me and Leah and that he can't let us get away from him.

And that's when he knelt on one knee and pulled a box out of the gift bag that my mom handed him. I instantly knew what was about to happen next, and I couldn't do anything but cry. This little brown box had the cutest little bow on it, and as he opened the box, I saw a huge diamond ring. As I heard the words, "Will you marry me?" I began

Jumping Ahead (Mia)

to cry even more because this was the ring that I wanted way back in high school when Luke and I would talk about our wedding plans. I would always show him the exact wedding ring that I wanted, but I couldn't believe after all these years he remembered the ring I always wanted. As I sat there crying with the man of my dreams holding a huge ring in front of me, my daughter grabbed the ring and said, "Yes, Mommy! Say yes, Mommy!" I burst into laughter and as I said yes, Leah and Luke put the ring on my finger together. My parents had the biggest smiles I had ever seen, and Luke's parents had the fakest smiles ever, but I didn't care. I was finally getting pieces of my dream back.

Chapter 8

Imperfect Dreams

Time flew by so fast; we got married, and I used the insurance money that I got from Liam's death to buy a house. Liam was very wise with money; he had policies already set up for me and Leah, and he even had her college funds already set aside. I was thankful for that. Luke's parents introduced us to a high-profile realtor, and she helped us find a beautiful home in the suburbs of Dallas, Texas. We got settled in the house, and then the journey began. Luke started grad school, and it was a very long and frustrating four years. I felt alone many nights because he was always gone. He was either in class, studying with his study group, researching with partners of his father's company, or sleeping. I was tired of feeling alone.

Luke helped his father at his law firm to get extra money while he was in medical school. We had money to take care of ourselves, but he wanted more so we could save. I expressed to him how I just wanted to spend more time with him, but he felt like I was just nagging, and I hated that so much. Leah even felt distant from Luke because he was focused on everything else. The more we argued, the more I started to feel a distance, and it also caused a gap between Leah and Luke's relationship. I even asked him to spend more time with Leah, and he would for a little while, but then he would be too busy again. I kept telling him that she would resent him for it, but he always took it as though I were saying that he was a bad father. At moments I did feel like he was a bad father because he didn't give her the attention that she needed. Children need attention, time, love, protection, and so much more from their fathers, but he thought that I was looking down on him as a father.

We ended up arguing about my past and how he felt like I regretted being with him and how I probably wished that Liam was still alive, which was partially true. I didn't regret marrying him, but I did miss Liam. I knew Liam would have been the perfect husband and father. I started throwing it in his face that Liam was better. I knew that what I said hurt Luke, but I thought that it would make him change. My plan failed because he started being even more distant, and he even started sleeping in our guest room. Leah noticed that we weren't sleeping in the same room, and she began asking questions. She didn't understand what was going on, but she knew that it wasn't right, and at that point, I realized things needed to change.

I called my parents and asked them to give us marriage counseling because we were falling apart. My dream of this perfect marriage and perfect life was crumbling right in front of me, and I was allowing it to happen. We started counseling, and at first, it was rocky, but then things started to change. Luke started to go to church more, and he started to spend more time at home with us. And as he came closer to his graduation from medical school, his faith in God started to go deeper. Luke started going to church every Sunday, even if I didn't want to go. I was amazed at how committed to God Luke was becoming. Our marriage was better, our sex life was back on track, and he even started doing more with Leah.

Leah was ten years old when Luke graduated from med school, and at that point, she was more interested in her friends than being at home with us. Luke started his residency, and he did that for three years. When he finally started working in his practice, Leah was thirteen, going on fourteen years old, I was pregnant with our son Micah, and our life was busy again. Leah was more interested in hanging out with her friends or doing activities in school. She was excited about the birth of her little brother, and she helped me with him a lot. The most Leah stayed home was when she was spending time with Micah, and I didn't complain, because they started forming an unbreakable bond.

Once I had Micah, Luke took paternity leave for a month and then went back to work. He worked twelve-hour shifts at the hospital, and I started feeling frustrated again. I felt like I was the only one taking care of Micah because Luke always had to work, and it started to overwhelm me. Don't get me wrong; Luke helped when he was at home, and he asked to pray together, but I always turned him down. I got to a point of not caring anymore. I didn't care about spending time with him, I didn't care about my marriage anymore—or about being a housewife anymore.

The Strawberry Seeds

When Micah turned five years old, he started kindergarten, and I joined a gym to start getting my body and mind back on track. Leah started college and moved to California. I went to this gym every day after I would drop Micah off to school. I got so fond of going to the gym that I decided to be a yoga instructor, and I loved it. One day as I was leaving the gym, I heard a deep voice say, "Well, well, well, nice to see you, Mia." As I turned to see who was speaking to me, I recognized a familiar face. "Oh my Gosh! Kyle! What are you doing here?" I yelled in excitement.

I couldn't believe Kyle was standing in front of me, all grown up. He was sexier than when we were kids, with dark brown curly hair with the sides faded, sexy hazel eyes, with one dimple on his left cheek. As I looked at him in amazement, he gave me a hug and told me how he was glad to see me. We both stood there apparently checking each other out because we were silent for at least a minute or two. When finally he broke the silence and asked if I wanted to get coffee and catch up, I felt butterflies in my stomach, and it reminded me of the days when we were kids. I always got butterflies around Kyle, he was so cute as a kid and even hotter as a grown man. That made me more nervous to be around him.

We went to get coffee and caught up on each other's lives. He told me that Kaley was getting married and moving to Europe with her soon-to-be husband. I was so happy to hear that she was doing well because over the years we slowly lost contact. I found out a lot about Kyle that day, and I was glad we had crossed paths. I found out that Kyle played professional football, he was single with no children, and he always had a crush on me since we were kids. I was shocked to hear that because it seemed like he was interested in girls who were his age only. This was the first of many more meetings that we had together.

Kyle and I exchanged numbers, and decided to keep in touch. We started out texting casually, and then it started becoming more frequent and flirtier. I was having issues in my marriage because my husband was always gone, and when he was home, we never really did anything together. So I started doing more with Kyle. We would meet up and have lunch together, we worked out at the gym together, and we even went on trips together. I wanted attention from my husband, but instead Kyle gave me that. My husband thought that I was going on trips with my yoga buddies, but I really was going with Kyle.

Kyle bought me whatever I wanted. Kyle knew that I was married, but we just couldn't stay away from each other. The first time we cheated was when we met up at his house to work out. Instead of working out in his home gym, we ended up working out in his bed. We couldn't stay away from each other after that day. I would turn into a whole new person when Kyle was around because I would try all kinds of things with him. He would take me shopping, he bought clothes for Micah, and he even bought me a dog. Oh, if you're wondering, I told my husband my yoga buddies got that dog for me as a gift.

Kyle was very sweet, and I know you are probably wondering whether I brought him around my children? No, I did not bring him around my kids, I didn't want them to know anything. Leah was busy, away in California, so she didn't even notice me being so busy. Micah was always with his cousins over at his auntie Mary Anne's house. Luke didn't notice anything unusual because he was always working. Kyle was my escape from reality.

Chapter 9

Digging Deep (Luke)

I was a man just trying to reach my goals as well as providing for my family. I wanted the best for Leah and Mia. Mia always made me feel like I was not doing good enough and compared me to Liam. She made me feel like less of a man. She started making me feel like I was the worst husband and father for trying to make a great life for our family. I wanted Leah to be able to go to private schools and have whatever she wanted, and I wanted Mia to be able to go back to school without the stress of finances. But instead, I got smacked in the face by being compared to her ex-husband.

I finished medical school and residency, and I thought that things would get better, but they didn't. I even started

The Strawberry Seeds

going to church again and getting myself right with God to please Mia, but that still didn't work. Mia was never satisfied. She knew what she was signing up for before she married me. She knew that I was going to school to be a surgeon. I just wanted to make Mia happy, but apparently, I still couldn't do that.

I began to pray to God and develop a deeper relationship with God. While I was working, I would pray over my family, and I would even read my Bible during down times. Mia became pregnant with Micah, and that just filled my heart with joy. We finally had our first child together, and it was a little boy. I didn't want to name him Luka because it reminded me of the younger versions of us, and I didn't want that. I wanted new memories of us. Micah was a name I found in the Bible. He was a prophet, and he was used by God. I wanted my son to have a powerful name and to be used by God in a great way.

Micah was the perfect mix of me and Mia. I think he looks a lot more like Mia then me, but it's fine with me because she makes beautiful babies. Leah and Micah are the perfect creations from my beautiful wife. Things seemed to get better for a little while after Micah came because Leah was home more, and Mia seemed happy.

Digging Deep (Luke)

When Micah turned five, Mia started going to the gym, and then she started really feeling confident and strong. She trained and then took classes to become a yoga instructor.

Mia started going to the gym more often and became so consumed with her classes that she was barely home. We started becoming more distant to each other and to the kids as well. Our house was very dysfunctional, and I hated my life. Since my wife and I seemed so distant, I began to get closer to God. The closer I got to God, the closer it seemed my wife was getting to her yoga buddies. Eventually, she was going on trips with them, and I was too tired to try to go. Her buddies liked her so much that they even bought her a dog that she had been wanting for years.

As a man, I felt like my wife was slipping out of my grasp, and it stung. I wanted my life to be better. I started setting money aside and putting them into stocks. I was trying to build our money. I began maximizing our income and saving money for my private practice and money for the kids to go to college. Liam had started working on Leah's before he died, but I wanted to make sure it would be enough for her once she graduated from high school.

The Strawberry Seeds

I was trying to set my family up for success. God was giving me ideas to start me on practice because I wanted to quit being a surgeon. I wanted to have my own private practice so I could work regular office hours. My goal was to start being at home with my family more. Through the instructions from God, my way was becoming clearer. My next hurdle was to rebuild my marriage and my relationship with my children.

It didn't help that my parents still didn't like Mia because they felt like she wasn't good enough. Through all the years we've been together, they still made reasons to not like her. They didn't like that she was a stay-at-home mom, they didn't like her relying on me, and they didn't like that she cheated on me and had Leah. My parents felt like it was fate for us to split when she had Leah and to never get back together. They were angry when I proposed to Mia, but I didn't care, because I loved her.

There were moments where I felt like I had made a huge mistake marrying her. There were moments where I wanted to just totally walk away, but she had already bought the house, and I didn't want to abandon her and Leah. I stood up for Mia, even when my parents badgered me about jumping into marriage so soon after graduating.

Digging Deep (Luke)

I never told her how many times they told me to divorce her, because I didn't want it to break her.

I felt like nothing I did was good enough for my parents or Mia. I felt like a failure in every area. I even felt like I was failing my kids. I feel like everything I ever wanted and dreamed about has turned into a living nightmare. What did I do to deserve this life? I'm not good enough for my parents, and I'm not good enough for my wife.

Apparently, my-in laws seem to see something special about me that no one else sees. The Hawthornes have been there for me since the time Mia and I began dating, and I thank God for them. There were many moments they stepped up for me when my parents wouldn't. I remember when Mia went to Jamaica, and Mr. Hawthorne and I worked on the firepit. We grew closer, and I looked to him as a father figure because He would give me wisdom in every area. I remember them calling me when I found out about Mia cheating and getting pregnant. They called to pray with me and encourage me. They knew that Mia messed up, but they still looked at me like a son.

Mia's parents were my parents, even when Mia married Liam. I never told her how her parents would text me from time to time to check on me or to encourage me. They were a huge part of why I gave my life to God. They showed me what unconditional love is. When you meet people like that in life, you should never leave them. And that's why I made that decision to call Mia when Mrs. Hawthorne told me about Liam's death. I wanted to show Mia unconditional love the way her parents showed me unconditional love.

I've been having these vivid dreams of Mia's mom cheating on her dad. I can't seem to shake them, and it's like I've been having them more and more. I don't know why, because I don't believe Mrs. Hawthorne would do that to her husband; she loves him too much. I asked one of my friends who is good with interpreting dreams, and he keeps saying to look at my wife, but I don't think Mia would do that to me again after the hurt she inflicted on me before. Am I in denial, or should I really be worried? Is Mia really messing around with someone else, or is it the enemy trying to play with my mind? Maybe I should ask her to find out if my dreams are real or fake.

I don't know what I'm going to do if I find out that she's cheating. I don't know if my heart, my mind, or my soul could handle that again. These past fifteen-plus years have been centered on me, trying to make everything perfect

Digging Deep (Luke)

for Mia and our children. I didn't want Mia to ever look at anyone else again. I wanted to be everything that she saw in Liam plus more, but it seems like I just can't get it right. Mia held Liam to a high esteem, and that has made me feel less than a man. I need to know if Mia has been faithful or whether she is still the same as when she was young.

Chapter 10

When the Lights Come On (Mia)

As I lie here, resting in his arms, I can't help but to think about my family and how this could destroy everything if Luke finds out. Now I'm feeling guilty all over again. This is not the first time I have cheated on my husband, and I doubt it will be the last time. I know it's wrong, but at this moment, it feels so perfect and right. The crazy thing is that Luke and I will be celebrating our fifteen-year anniversary soon, and I don't really know how to feel about that.

Today I'm heading back home from Cancun, and this trip with Kyle was magical. From the time Luke and I have

When the Lights Come On (Mia)

been married, we have only been on three vacations. Our first was our honeymoon, our second was his sister's destination wedding in Africa, and we had one family trip for Leah's sweet sixteen birthday. Luke has been too busy working to even take me on a date right in our city. I am so ready to leave this marriage and start fresh with Kyle, but at the same time I love Luke and just want him to notice me. I just want him to see that I don't need money or a big home; I just want him. I want sweet conversations in bed before we go to sleep. I want fun picnics in the park while watching Micah play. I want random pop-ups on Leah while she's away at college. I just want my husband to spend time with me and his children. I just want the old spontaneous Luke back, the Luke who had surprises up his sleeve every time you turned around.

I rode with Kyle to his house to get my car. The entire time I was in Cancun, my car was at Kyle's place. Luke thought that I parked in the airport garage and went to Cancun to a yoga retreat. I've gotten pretty good at lying now. As we pulled up to Kyles's house, I decide to ask the question.

"Kyle, would you want to take things to the next level if I leave Luke?" That's when Kyle said with the weirdest expression on his face, "Mia, you know I'm not the serious type; I just like having an open field. That's why I love being with you because I knew that you would never leave Luke." And that was the most embarrassing moment I could have ever encountered. This man I had been having an affair with for almost a year never saw anything with me in the first place. He just used me, and whenever he finally gets tired of me, he will dispose of me with no remorse.

At that moment, I couldn't hold back my tears, because I was so humiliated. That's when he said the dumbest response ever. "Mia, don't cry. I'm not going anywhere anytime soon." At that moment, I realized that I was making a huge mistake and it was time to leave Kyle alone. He just liked the thrill of having sex with me and sneaking around but didn't have any feelings for me.

I wondered, *Why am I allowing this to happen when I have a man at home who does love me and is doing everything he can for me?* That's when my phone began to ring. I looked at my phone and quickly got myself together to answer my phone. To my surprise, it was Luke calling. "Hey honey!"

"Yeah, I just got back from Cancun. Oh, yes the trip was amazing!"

When the Lights Come On (Mia)

As I sat there staring at Kyle's nonchalant face, I was disgusted at the lies I was telling Luke. I couldn't believe I was about to throw fifteen years of marriage away for a dog. Right at that moment, I heard those daunting words, "I can't do this anymore, Mia. We need to talk when you get home." In that moment, I had a huge knot in my throat. Something within me knew that Luke had seen something or found out something, and I wasn't ready for the consequences. The only thing I could say was "Okay, honey. I'm on my way now." I immediately hung up the phone.

Kyle looked pissed and asked, "What was that about? I thought you were going to stay over for a little before you went home?" and that's when I just went off. "*Are you serious*? You just sat here and basically said that I was nothing more than just a fling to you and that you don't want me, but then when my husband is ready for me to come home, you want to get mad!" That's when Kyle tried to act dumb and said, "I didn't say that. I just said I'm not ready for anything serious, but I like you a lot." It pissed me off even more to hear those stupid words, "Like you a lot." I don't want to be liked, I want to be loved and appreciated.

Then I said, "Kyle, you just don't get it. I don't want to be liked; I want to be loved."

Kyle finally looked at me and said, "I don't love you, Mia. I just love having sex with you because I trust that you won't try to trap me by getting pregnant because of my being a football player. I knew since you were married, you wouldn't take chances like that."

And that's when I lost it even more. "So you're saying you used me for sex because you knew I wouldn't try to get pregnant by you! You're a disgusting human being; you probably had other women too! I feel so disgusting and used right now!" At that moment I burst into tears and screamed while covering my hands with my face.

Kyle said, "No, Mia, I only had you, and that's no lie; it was only me and you. I promise you I didn't have anyone else, but I just knew I could trust you, and that's what drew me to you sexually. You're a great woman, you're smart and caring, you're a wonderful mother, and a great friend, but I'm just not ready for commitment, and I thought that you would understand that." Kyle tried to hug me, but I just pushed him away and got out the car.

He tried to get out and grab me to comfort me, but that's when I said, "No, don't ever touch me again—it's

When the Lights Come On (Mia)

over! What we had is officially over, and I don't ever want to see or hear from you again!"

Then Kyle let me go and stepped back in disbelief as I got in the car and drove off. I was serious; I never wanted to see Kyle again because I was so hurt at what he did. I don't even remember my ride home, because my mind was so distraught. I was all over the place with my emotions that by the time I got home, I just knew it was about to get worse. And, boy, was I right. As I pulled in our driveway, chills began to come over my body. I got out the car, went into the house, and followed the sound of the TV into the living room. That's when I saw Luke sitting on the couch, and next to him were two huge duffle bags filled to the max. My heart dropped. I knew Luke had found out, but how?

"Hey, honey, what's all of this?" Luke looked at me with the most serious, yet tired look on his face and said, "This is me leaving and never coming back." I felt the tears welling up again, and this time, I really couldn't control myself.

I asked the dumb question, "Why are you leaving?"

Luke said those daunting words, "I know you've been cheating, Mia. I started having dreams about your parents when God began to show what you have been doing. At first, I was in denial, but after months of investigating, I found out you were cheating and not with anybody, but with my high school buddy Kyle. I can't even believe you would even do this to me again, let alone with one of my old high school friends." Luke was so calm it almost scared me. It made me realize how much I had really hurt him this time. I knew he was really done, and that made me feel like my heart was instantly ripped out of my chest. I knew I had messed up again and there was no turning back this time.

Luke is officially done with me, and I know there's nothing I can do or say to get him back, either. There was silence for a moment, and finally Luke stood up to leave. As he was grabbing his bag, he said, "I love you, Mia. I just hate that you don't see me the same way I see you. You're beyond special to me." And he walked past me, went down the hall to the garage, and left. I couldn't say anything; I just slid down the wall to the ground and cried into my knees.

I never thought I would be in this spot, but here I am.

Chapter 11

Pain Is Real

That night was the worst night of my life. I had lost Luke forever; he was the one I thought I would spend my forever with. Yet again, I was reckless and messed things up. A week went by, and Luke called only to check on Micah. Kyle called too, but I never answered. I resented everything that Kyle and I ever did. I didn't want any part of Kyle. I even blocked his number after two weeks.

Eventually, a month went by, and I still was hurting; I didn't know what to do, because I was lost. I wasn't working as a yoga instructor, because I was so busy running around with Kyle, so they replaced me with someone else. So once Luke left, I was stressed as to how I would even survive. Luke finally called to talk to me, and he

The Strawberry Seeds

said that he was going to help me pay the mortgage for the house, but I had to work to pay the bills. So I got a job working for my parents' church as an assistant.

My parents knew what happened because, as usual, they talk to Luke more than me. Luke told them everything, and of course, they called me, angrily, and wanted answers as to why I would do such a thing, but I didn't have an excuse. I was completely wrong, and I was ungrateful. I didn't appreciate Luke when I had him, and I regret that.

My parents offered me a job at the church, not so much because I could pay my bills but because I needed to be back in the church. I didn't object, either, because I knew I had messed up, and I didn't want to be punished anymore. I would see Luke at church because he was very close to my parents, and he was very active in their church. Months went by, and nothing changed until one day Luke stopped by to pick up Micah up for the weekend. What was unusual was the fact that he came hours before Micah got home from school. Luke wanted to talk about our divorce and how I felt about the custody decisions. I told him that I was fine with Micah wanting to stay with him because he is his father. Eventually, the conversation turned from talking about the divorce to talking about God and how we both began to get deeper relationships with God.

Luke and I had been separated for six months, and it was a trying time for me, but I drew closer to God like never before. I began to see things differently. I began to see my faults and the role that I played in our failed marriage. I was ready to accept my demons because I had a closet full of them. I was ready for God to change me inside and out because I was lost when Luke left me. I wanted to be better, so I chased after God and began to change. As I worked on myself, I began to understand why Luke was doing all that working. Luke was looking beyond himself; instead, he was trying to make the best life for us and our kids. He wanted them to have a bright future, and I regret not understanding that.

So that day, when Luke came early, that was my opportunity to apologize to him and tell him everything that I did wrong. I apologized for not being understanding, for cheating, and for never being the best wife I could be. We talked for hours, and before we knew it, Micah was home and ready to go with his dad. Luke didn't want to leave, but he knew Micah was looking forward to a fun weekend in Houston. We said our goodbyes, and as they left, I cried yet again because I knew Luke was the best thing I ever had. Luke loved me the way a man is designed to love his wife. Luke did the best he knew as a husband and father. I cried with ice cream and turned on romance movies.

Eleven o'clock came, and my phone began to ring. It was Luke calling, and I immediately began to worry because I thought something had happened. To my surprise, he called because he wanted to check on me. Luke called to make sure I was doing okay. I hadn't had that from Luke in a long time, so it felt good to hear his concern for me. I was so excited to hear his voice on the phone, it brought tears to my eyes. Luke knew I was crying because he heard the shake in my voice. He immediately asked if I was okay, and the only thing I could say was "I love you so much, Luke!" In that moment, I never thought I would hear Luke say the same, but he did. He told me that he loved me, too, and that he had never stopped loving me.

We talked for hours about our faults and where we went wrong. For the first time we both shared with each other our personal issues that we struggled with. I had issues that were in me that stemmed from my childhood, and they stayed with me into adulthood. We realized that we had baggage that we carried on and had never dealt with. Finally,

PAIN IS REAL

we were getting the healing we needed by expressing our hurts and pains from childhood. The seed of hurt can cause other seeds to form as well. Through getting a relationship with God, He began to show us the wounds that we had in our hearts that damaged us as adults.

Luke was never good enough for his parents, so he grew up trying to prove to everyone that he could reach any goal he set, but in turn, it damaged relationships around him. Mia grew up in a strict, God-fearing home, and when she finally broke out, she wanted to experience life. However, through rejection, she would try to suppress her hurt through sex and men. Luke and Mia realized that they were damaged when they took that six-month long break from each other. God had to take them on a spiritual journey to find who they are and *whose* they are. Finally, when Luke got back from Houston with Micah, he asked Mia on a date the following weekend. They began to start their marriage over by dating again, and eventually, Luke moved back into the house, and they made a lot of changes. Mia did everything in her power to show Luke that she was faithful, and Luke did everything in his power to be present more often. When Micah turned eight, Mia and Luke had a baby girl named Selah.

Selah

Joy after the Storm

---

*S*elah is a pause, and that's exactly why they named her that because they had a pause in their marriage. That pause was for them to get close to God and to find themselves in Him, during which time they got closer to God and got the inner healing they needed. Once that pause was over, God blessed them with a beautiful baby girl. Selah was the final and complete addition to their family. Selah drew Mia and Luke closer than they ever would have imagined.

Have you ever been through issues in life that you never thought you would come through? That's what happened to Mia and Luke; they were human, and humans fail. We are not perfect, sometimes we mess up, sometimes we fall short, and sometimes we don't deserve grace. God is always ready for us, but we are not always ready to surrender to Him. The storms are designed to make us stronger and to draw us closer to God. Sometimes we must separate from friends, family, or spouses to get what God wants us to develop inside of us.

The Strawberry Seeds

❦

A strawberry is technically a cluster fruit containing seeds on the outside. There are many individual seeds on the outside of the whole strawberry. Think of the strawberry as your heart, and you have seeds that have formed on the outside, which have clustered together. That is the same as our hearts. We develop seeds on the outside of our heart, and we let them sit and eventually cluster our hearts with hatred, jealousy, low self-esteem, insecurities, anger, commitment issues, and so much more. When a bad seed takes root in your heart, it can become rotten, and then it can begin to form more bad seeds.

The strawberry is a delicate plant, and when caring for it, you must know what you are doing. You can put the plant in the wrong soil, and it can wither and die, or you could water it too much, and it would rot. The plant

THE STRAWBERRY SEEDS

is delicate, and that is exactly like our hearts. We have delicate hearts, and God wants us to make sure we protect them and keep them free of rotten attitudes and ways. God wants us to have a pure heart so He can take root and plant love down in us. That is what He did with Mia and Luke. God planted love down on the inside of them. That seed of love formed into unconditional love.

God wants to uproot every bad seed in your heart so He can plant the seed of love down on the inside of you. God is ready for you to experience love and life in a whole new way. Let God come into your heart, your life, and your situation and transform it into something beautiful.

The Lord gave me strawberry seeds because when I was a teenager, my dad brought me some strawberry seeds to grow. I planted them, and they began to sprout and grow, but the pot I had them in was getting too small, and they needed a bigger one. When I got a bigger pot, I needed more soil, and when my dad got more soil for it, he ended up getting manure instead of potting soil, and it killed my precious strawberries. I didn't understand why that happened until years later, when the Lord brought it back to me at a time when I was going into surgery for a cyst. (That's another story to come.) The Lord showed

The Strawberry Seeds

me that He planted seeds of love in me, but my hurts and pains down through the years caused other seeds to form. The seeds of low self-esteem, shame, and trust issues were some of the seeds that formed in my heart. I was bruised and burned by people I trusted the most, and that scarred me until God was ready for all of that to come out. For me to flourish, God needed those bad seeds that were planted to come out.

God was ready for the seed of unconditional love to take root and grow in me. My journey of unconditional love wasn't easy, but I learned to love the unlovable. I learned to love people who were aiming to destroy me and my character.

to be continued

Thank you for reading my book and being a support. I pray that you have been blessed by this book and that the seed of love would take root into your heart. I pray that God will do a transformation in your life that you never saw coming. Stay tuned for more because a sequel is coming. We are going to dig into the story of Leah.

Thank you.

Love,

Ciera

CPSIA information can be obtained
at www.ICGtesting.com
Printed in the USA
BVHW051357240722
642894BV00005B/97

9 781662 851001